Dear Junior Gymnast:

I'm Dominique Dawes, and I love gymnastics! When I was six years old, I spent all my time tumbling around the house and jumping on furniture. So my parents decided to sign me up for gymnastics.

Even though it was their idea for me to take lessons, my mom and dad let me decide whether I wanted to be a serious gymnast or not. They never made me go to the gym — but they always took me there when I wanted to go. And I thought gymnastics was so much fun that I went almost every day!

In this book, Katie Magee finds out that having fun is the most important part of being a great gymnast!

And I hope you have fun reading Katie's story!

Dominique Dawes

Katie's Gold Medal

JUNIOR GYMNASTS

Katie's Gold Medal

BY TEDDY SLATER

illustrated by Wayne Alfano

A
LITTLE APPLE
PAPERBACK

SCHOLASTIC INC.
New York Toronto London Auckland Sydney

A PARACHUTE PRESS BOOK

ISBN 0-590-95987-5

12 11 10 9 8 7 6 5 4 3 2 1   6 7 8 9/9 0 1/0

Printed in the U.S.A.   40

First Scholastic printing, December 1996

For my husband, Fred

Contents

Katie's Gold Medal

Good News!

"Tickets! Come and get 'em! Step right up and say how many!"

Coach Jody laughed as our whole gymnastics team jumped up from the mats and crowded around her. I got there first.

"Whoa, Katie!" Coach Jody cried. "Calm down, everyone!" she went on. "The meet isn't until a week from Saturday. Maybe you should all sit back down and *I'll* come to *you*!"

Coach Jody fanned the yellow tickets out in her hand, and my teammates and I plopped onto the mats again. Our two-hour

Thursday workout was over, but no one wanted to leave. We were way too excited. The tickets were for the Springfield Invitational Level 5 Gymnastics Meet!

Level 5 is when gymnasts first start competing. My team has already been in one meet. But that was in Riverdale, an hour away from Springfield. This meet is going to be right here — at Jody's Gym! — so our friends and families can all come see us.

Coach Jody bent down and held the tickets out to me. "Just one for you. Right, Katie?" she asked.

"Uh-huh," I said, jumping to my feet. It's hard to stay sitting down when Coach Jody is standing up. Coach Jody is over six feet tall, and I'm exactly three feet eleven and three-quarter inches! That makes me the shortest girl on the team. I'm also the youngest — eight and a half. And I'm the only one with divorced parents. That's how come I only needed one ticket!

Coach Jody smiled as she handed it to me. "One for Katie Magee," she said, crossing my name off the list on her clipboard. Then she moved on to Amanda Calloway. Amanda's yellow leotard was the same exact color as the tickets.

"How many for you, Amanda?" Coach Jody asked.

"Six, please," Amanda answered.

"Sorry, kiddo. These tickets are just for your family," Coach Jody said. "Your friends will have to get their own."

"These *are* for my family!" Amanda declared.

Coach Jody gently tugged Amanda's dark brown braid. "Oops!" She chuckled. "I don't know how I forgot *that*."

"There are a lot of them to remember," Amanda agreed.

Amanda has a mother, a father, two sisters, one brother, a grandmother, and seven pets — one for each person. They all live together in a big house on Cranberry Street. Amanda is my best friend, and the Calloways are my favorite family! It must be so much fun to be part of a big family like that.

As soon as Amanda took her tickets, Dana Lewis jumped up. Dana is my other best friend. She just has a regular-sized family — a mother, a father, a little brother, and a dog. They all have red hair and blue eyes, just like Dana. Except for the dog!

"Three for me," Dana told Coach Jody.

"That I know," Coach Jody said, handing the tickets to Dana.

Without asking, she gave tickets to the other girls — three to Hannah Rose Crenshaw, four to Liz Halsey, and another three to Emily Stone. Amanda only moved to town last fall, but the rest of us have been taking lessons here for years. Coach Jody has known us all since we were little!

★ ★ ★

After I changed back into my school clothes, I followed Amanda and Dana out to the bike rack. We always ride our bikes home together.

Before I had a chance to climb on my bike, Dana jumped on hers. "Race you to the Good-bye Tree!" she hollered as she zoomed off ahead of us.

Amanda got on her bike and pedaled after her. Dana and Amanda really like to compete with each other. They're the two best gymnasts on our team, but they each want to be the *only* best one!

I don't care about winning as much as they do. But I jumped on my bike, too. I didn't want to be left behind.

We were all out of breath by the time we caught up to Dana at the big oak tree at Cranberry and Sixth. That's where Amanda and I turn left and Dana turns right. Before we say good-bye, we always stop and talk — mostly about gymnastics and school.

Amanda and I go to Washington Elementary School. I'm in third grade and she's in fourth. Dana's in fourth grade, too, but she goes to Lincoln Elementary.

Today no one felt like talking about school, though. We were too excited about the meet. We leaned our bikes against the tree and plopped down on the grass.

"I hope I do as well as I did at the last meet!" I told my friends. I still couldn't believe I had won a bronze medal at my very first competition.

"I hope I do *better*," Amanda said.

"Me, too!" Dana exclaimed.

"You guys are greedy," I teased. Amanda won two gold medals at the Riverdale meet, and Dana got one gold and one silver. "You're never satisfied."

"That's right!" Dana and Amanda yelled together. Then they both laughed.

"You know what I wish?" Amanda asked. "I wish Coach Jody would let me wear my purple leotard for the meet."

Dana snatched the yellow ribbon out of Amanda's hair. "Oh, A-*man*-da!" she groaned. "You are so superstitious."

Amanda grabbed back her ribbon. She smoothed her long yellow sweater down over her matching yellow skirt. "I am not!" she said. But she is.

Amanda has a different lucky color for every day of the week. Everything she wears has to be that same color — even her underpants! Thursday is yellow, and Saturday is supposed to be purple. Too bad the meets are always on Saturdays — and our uniforms are red! Amanda only wants to wear red on *Sundays*.

"Well," I said, "Coach Jody will never let you wear purple. We all have to look the same — we're a team! Why don't you just wear your purple barrette like you did last time?"

Amanda shrugged. "I will," she said.

"But it would be luckier if *everything* could be purple."

"Oh, A-*man*-da!" Dana groaned again.

"Hey, do you know what would make *me* feel lucky?" I said.

"What?" Amanda asked.

"If my dad could be here for the meet," I said.

"I thought he *was* coming," Dana said.

"Not for another week and a half," I told her. "Not in time to see me compete."

When my parents got divorced last year, my dad moved to another house in Springfield so I could still see him all the time. But five months ago, he had to go to Mexico for his job. We've been writing to each other ever since, and he calls me two times a week. But it isn't the same. I miss him a lot.

"I can't believe I've never met your dad," Amanda exclaimed. "He must have left right before I moved here. Was he really a gymnast, too?"

"Yup," I told her. "In college. He's the one who got me into gymnastics. It would be so cool if he could come to the meet."

"Well, soon he'll be home for good," Amanda said. "Then he can come to all your meets!"

"That's right," I agreed. Suddenly I felt much better. "I've got to go now," I told my friends. "I have a ton of homework tonight."

"Me, too," Dana said.

"Me three," Amanda chimed in.

We all climbed onto our bikes. Then we yelled good-bye at the same time, and we rode away from the Good-bye Tree.

I was wheeling my bike into the garage when I heard a car horn.

HONK, HONK, A-HONK, HONK! . . . HONK! HONK!

I didn't even have to turn around to know who it was. My mother always honks like that. She knocks that way, too. When I was little I thought it was a secret signal — like a password — just between the two of us. Now I know better. But I still smile every time she does it.

As Mom slowly turned into our driveway, I leaned my bike against the house and ran to meet her.

"Good news!" she announced, getting out of the car. "Your father called me at work this afternoon. He said to tell you that he's coming home this Monday instead of next Monday. He can't wait another week to see you!"

I threw my arms around my mother's waist. "Daddy's coming *this* Monday?" I shrieked. "That's the best news in the whole world! He'll be here for my gymnastics meet!"

2
The List

It was still dark when I woke up Monday morning. I looked at the clock on my night table and grinned. Five forty-nine A.M. In less than twelve hours my dad would be home!

I felt much too excited to sleep, but I closed my eyes anyway. I pictured me and my dad doing all the fun things we used to do. All the things we hadn't done for five whole months!

I sat up and reached under my mattress for my journal and a pen. I always put them there before I go to sleep — just in case I get a super-smart idea in the middle of the night.

I opened my journal to the first empty page. On the very top line, in big letters, I wrote:

THINGS TO DO WITH DADDY!

For a minute I couldn't think what to write next. There were so many things I wanted to do with him. I finally decided to pick one special thing for each day of the week.

By the time I finished writing my list, it was seven o'clock. I had to hurry to get ready for school. I looked at the list one last time before I got out of bed. I knew that I was going to have a great week with my dad.

MONDAY - Sleep Over at his house

TUESDAY - Go to the Zoo

WEDNESDAY - Make Kitchen Sink
            Pizza

THURSDAY - Dog Show at Springfield
            Arena

FRIDAY - Rollerblading

SATURDAY - My Gymnastics Meet!!!!!

SUNDAY - Picnic in the park

I stared at the clock all day long.
Usually I like school. But today it dragged
on and on. I thought three o'clock would
never come!

Gymnastics was the same way. Practice
was only two hours long — just like it
always is. But it seemed so much longer

14

today! I was counting the hours until I would see my dad.

The minute practice ended, I ran into the locker room. I grabbed my boots and shoved my feet inside. By the time my friends came in, I was already ready to go. I threw my jacket on over my leotard and headed for the door. Dana and Amanda laughed as I hurried past them.

"Hey — aren't you forgetting something?" Amanda called.

I stopped at the door and spun around. "What?" I asked.

"Your clothes," Dana replied.

I looked at my locker. The door hung open and my school clothes were all stuffed inside. "Oops," I said, grabbing my clothes and shoving them into my gym bag. "Thanks!" I added as I started off.

"Hey! What about *us*?" Amanda cried.

I stopped again. "Sorry!" I said. "I can't wait for you guys today. My dad's plane landed at four o'clock, and he promised to come straight to our house. He's probably there now!"

"Okay — see you tomorrow," Amanda said.

"Say hi to your dad for me," Dana called as I hurried out.

"Thanks," I yelled back. "I will."

I couldn't believe it — I was finally going to see Dad!

My parents were sitting in the kitchen when I burst through the door. Daddy jumped up from the table and hugged me so hard I almost couldn't breathe. It felt wonderful!

After a while he let go and took a big step back. "Katie!" he cried. "Look at you! My little girl is all grown-up!"

Mom looked from me to Dad and back again. "I forgot how much she looks like you," she said to him.

"Except for the green eyes," he replied. "Those are definitely yours."

"But it's *your* blond hair," Mom said.

Then they smiled at each other.

My parents used to fight a lot. But the minute they got divorced, they started getting along really well.

For a few seconds we all just stared at one another. Now that Dad was actually here, I didn't know what to say to him.

"Why don't you take your father up to your room and introduce him to Speedy?" Mom finally suggested.

"Speedy?" Daddy raised an eyebrow. "Who's that?"

I grabbed my dad's hand and pulled him toward the stairs. "He's my turtle!" I told him. "I'll show you."

When we got up to my room, Speedy was fast asleep on a lettuce leaf in his tank. I tapped his shell with my finger, and he stuck his head out.

"Daddy," I said, "this is Speedy. Speedy, this is Dad."

My dad said hi to Speedy, but I could tell he wasn't that interested in him. Most people aren't. *I* love Speedy, though. I wish I could have a dog or cat, too, but my mom's allergic to them.

As soon as Speedy went back in his shell, I picked up my journal and handed it to Dad. "Look what I wrote this morning," I said. I pointed to my THINGS TO DO WITH DADDY! list.

"This is quite a list," Dad said when he finished reading it. "But we don't have to do everything this week. Now that I'm back, we'll have lots of time together."

"I know," I said happily.

Dad put my journal down and walked around the room, looking at all my things. He smiled when he got to the desk and saw my pencil case. It's shaped like a shark with shiny zipper teeth. Dad gave it to me on my first day of kindergarten. I've lost it a million times since then. But I always find it again.

Dad picked up the case and stuck his finger into the shark's mouth. Then he tried to tug his finger out, pretending the shark was biting him. The first time he did that, I thought it would really eat him. I was only five then, so it made me cry. This time I just laughed and grabbed my pencil case back.

Dad laughed, too.

"Do you still have all those pen pals?" he asked.

"Fourteen of them in eleven different countries," I replied. "Not counting you!"

"Well, you and I aren't pen pals anymore," Dad said. "I'm back for good. From now on, when we have something to tell each other we can say it face-to-face."

"Hurray!" I could hardly believe I was actually talking to my dad — in person!

"Now can we go to your house?" I asked. "Mom said I could sleep over tonight."

"You sure can," he replied.

While I packed my overnight bag, Dad moved to my desk and picked up my gymnastics medal. "Is this the medal you wrote me about?" he asked.

"Yup!" I said proudly. "It's real bronze. I got it for being third on balance beam."

"Not bad!" Dad said. "I can't wait for your meet on Saturday. I bet you'll win a *gold* medal then! Right, honey?"

"A gold?" I said nervously. "I don't know if I can."

"Sure you can!" he told me. "I'll help you!"

Daddy headed out the door. "We can start tonight," he called over his shoulder. "Let's go!"

He can't really expect me to win a gold medal, I thought as I hurried after him. *Can* he?

3
Un-Listed

BOIING! Dana bounced up. "Are you okay, Katie?" she yelled.

SPROIING! Amanda bounced down. "You look sad," she added.

Then — *BOIING! SPROIING!* — Amanda went up and Dana came down.

"You guys! Cut it out!" I cried. "You're making me dizzy."

It was Tuesday afternoon. Dana, Amanda, and I were hanging out in Dana's backyard. Dana was supposed to be watching her little brother, Freddy, but she and

Amanda were fooling around on the trampoline. I was the one who was actually watching Freddy.

Dana's dog, Woof, sat in the grass next to me. Suddenly she jumped up and ran over to Dana. Freddy followed her. They both climbed onto the trampoline.

Dana giggled. "Okay, Katie, we'll stop," she said. "It's getting too crowded up here anyway." She and Amanda jumped off and dropped down on the ground with me.

"So what's up?" Dana asked. "How come you're so quiet today?"

"I'm okay," I said. "I'm just tired. I stayed at my dad's house last night and we went to sleep really late."

"I almost forgot!" Dana cried. "Your dad came home! How was it? How is he? Did you have a great time?" Before I could even answer, she asked, "Did you show him your list?"

"Uh-huh," I said. "He's really excited about coming to the meet. He thinks I'm going to win a gold medal."

"Cool!" Amanda said. "You're lucky your dad used to be a gymnast. He can teach you all kinds of tricks."

"I guess so," I answered.

"You don't sound very excited," Dana said. "What's the matter?"

"Nothing really," I told her. "It's just that last night at Dad's I wanted to hear all about Mexico and tell him about school and stuff. But all *he* wanted to talk about was the meet. He really wants me to win."

"You already said that," Dana pointed out.

"I know," I said. "That's because *Dad* kept saying it. He wanted to see my floor routine. And then when I showed him, he kept correcting me and making me do it over. He's so picky."

Amanda's big brown eyes opened

24

wide. "Did he yell at you?" she asked.

"Nope," I said. "He did something even worse."

"What?" both my friends said at once.

"He videotaped my whole floor routine!" I exclaimed. "Then he made me watch it while he pointed out everything I did wrong. He said his college coach used to do that all the time."

"So what's wrong with that?" Dana asked. "It sounds like fun."

"It made me really nervous," I said.

"I'd *love* to be videotaped," Amanda chimed in. "It wouldn't make *me* nervous."

"Nothing makes you nervous," I told her.

"Well, everything makes *you* nervous!" Amanda teased me.

"That's not true!" I giggled. "The trampoline doesn't. Look!"

I got up and ran over to the trampoline. Freddy was still jumping up and down on it. Woof jumped up every time Freddy landed.

"Katie!" Freddy hollered. "Come bounce with us." Woof barked.

As soon as I climbed onto the trampoline, Freddy scooped up Woof and handed her to me. I jumped up and down with the dog in my arms. It was fun. Then Dana and Amanda squeezed on, and we all fell down in a heap.

Everyone was laughing and barking so loud that I didn't even hear the car stop out front. But Woof did. Suddenly, she jumped out of my arms and raced across the yard. The rest of us followed her out to the sidewalk.

When we got there, my dad was just getting out of his car.

"This is some welcoming committee," he said as we all crowded around him. "Hi, Dana. It's good to see you again. You, too,

Woof," he added, bending down to pat her. "Remember me?"

Dad laughed when Woof licked his face. "I guess she does," he said. He seemed so happy, I didn't want to tell him Woof does that to everyone.

"How about you, Freddy?" Dad said. But Freddy got shy all of a sudden and hid behind Dana. Then my father turned to Amanda.

"And you must be Amanda," he said, putting out his hand. "Katie wrote me all about you."

Amanda shook his hand and said, "How do you do, Mr. Magee?" Amanda has perfect manners. She always says "please" and "thank you" — even to her friends.

As soon as Amanda shook hands with Daddy, Freddy decided he wanted to shake, too. Then Woof stuck out her paw. That's her only trick, and she loves doing it. Daddy shook with both of them. Then he made

believe he was going to shake my hand —
but he kissed it instead.

"Daddy!" I giggled. "What are you
doing here?"

"You'll never guess," he said with a
smile.

"Umm . . . we're going to the zoo?" I
asked.

"Uh-uh," he said, still smiling. "Better
than that."

"The dog show!" I cried, jumping up
and down in excitement. I felt like I was still
on the trampoline.

"Nope," Dad said. "You're not even
close."

"What?" I asked.

"Well," he answered, "I called Coach
Jody and asked if you could have an extra
workout this afternoon!"

I looked at Dana and Amanda. They
were both staring at my father. "But today is
Tuesday," I protested. "We don't do gym-

nastics on Tuesdays. We do it Mondays, Wednesdays, and Thursdays."

"I know," Dad said. "But this will be a private session — just you and me. Coach Jody is working with the Level Six team in the big gym, but she said you can use the little gym — as long as I'm there to spot you. Isn't that great?" he exclaimed.

"I guess so," I said. "But what about my list? We're supposed to go to the zoo. The polar bear had three babies last month, and I still haven't seen them!"

"We'll have plenty of time for bears after the meet," my dad replied.

I didn't say anything. I love gymnastics, but I really wanted to go to the zoo. I didn't have room for extra practices on my list.

"Come on, honey. It will be great!" Daddy said. "And with a little extra practice, you'll be way ahead of the other girls."

"*Daddy!*" I squealed. I couldn't believe

he said that with Dana and Amanda standing right there!

"Oops! Nothing personal," Dad said as my friends began to giggle. That only made them laugh harder. And even though I was totally embarrassed, I had to laugh, too.

The only trouble was, I could tell my dad was serious!

The Ugliest Leo
in the World

Amanda stepped into her navy-blue leotard. Then she tied her hair back with a matching ribbon. It was Wednesday afternoon at Jody's Gym — Amanda's blue day. Amanda, Dana, Emily, Liz, and I were in the locker room, putting on our gym clothes.

"So how was practice with your dad yesterday?" Amanda asked me.

"I can't believe you're trying to get more practice than the rest of us!" Dana chimed in. "No fair, Katie!" she went on. "If your father keeps helping, you'll win every medal at the meet!"

I felt my cheeks grow hot. "Oh, no!" I gasped. "You know I didn't want to practice yesterday. I — "

I stopped talking as my friends began to giggle.

"It's okay, Katie," Amanda said. "Dana's only teasing. We both think it's great that you want to win."

"But I *don't*," I wailed. "I mean, I *do*. But I really wanted to go to the zoo yesterday! Dad and I are already a whole day behind on my things-to-do list. *He's* the one who wants me to get extra gymnastics practice."

"I still think it's great," Amanda said. "You're lucky your father cares about the meet. It shows he cares about you."

I wriggled into my faded black leo and shrugged. "That's what Mom says."

There was a squeak from one of the

toilet stalls in the bathroom alcove. The door opened and Hannah Rose's head popped out. "You should always listen to your mother," Hannah Rose said in her usual bossy way. Then she pulled her head back into the stall and closed the door with another squeak.

Dana rolled her eyes. But Amanda ignored Hannah Rose. "Your dad just wants you to win," she went on. "And I bet you will. If you practice really hard, you'll definitely get another bronze medal."

"Maybe," I said. "But Dad keeps talking about the *gold* medals."

"Wait a minute!" Dana cried. "The gold ones are all supposed to be *mine*!"

"Says who?" Amanda demanded.

"Just kidding!" Dana said. Then she started to giggle.

I giggled, too, but Amanda didn't. Amanda never jokes about winning. "Is your dad giving you another practice session tonight?" she asked me.

"No way!" I yelped. "We're going to make dinner at his house and then we're going to the zoo. It's open late on Wednesdays."

I pulled my journal out of my gym bag and turned to the list. "See," I told Dana. "By the time I go to sleep tonight, we'll be right back on schedule."

Amanda peeked over my shoulder. "What's a Kitchen Sink Pizza?"

"It's my dad's special recipe," I explained. "He calls it that because we put in everything but the kitchen sink. We start with English muffins and tomato sauce and then we pile a whole lot of other weird stuff on top."

"Like what?" Liz asked.

"Well, we mostly just have cheese and mushrooms and peppers and onions," I said.

"That doesn't sound too weird to me," Hannah Rose put in. She began washing her hands. "It just sounds like a regular pizza."

"Well, Dad once put pickles on his," I told her. "And I once tried marshmallows."

"Marshmallows!" Emily gagged. "Yuck!"

"Well, it *was* kind of gross," I admitted. "But it was better than the pickles."

"Your father sounds like fun," Liz said.

"He is," I agreed. "He's the best dad in the world!"

Dad's car was parked outside the gym when I left at 5:30. I waved good-bye to my friends and ran over to it.

"Hi, Daddy," I said as he rolled down the window and stuck his head out for a kiss. "How come you're here? I'm supposed to go to your house."

Daddy leaned across the seat and

opened the passenger door. "Hop in and I'll tell you," he said.

I pointed to the bicycle rack. "What about my bike?"

"You can leave it there for now," he said. "We'll pick it up on the way back from the restaurant."

"The restaurant?" I repeated as I got into the car. "I thought we were making Kitchen Sink Pizza!"

"Not tonight," he said. "I have a much better idea."

A few minutes later we were sitting in a booth at Farmer Brown's Pizzeria.

"I never heard of a health-food pizza place," I said, looking around the restaurant. There were little white lace curtains on the windows and lots of plants. The place mats were shaped like vegetables. Mine was a giant eggplant. Dad's was a squash.

"It's new," my father said. "The food is supposed to be delicious — *and* healthy. If you want to be a champion, Katie, you have to take care of your body. That means no more junk food."

"Oh." I opened the menu. Everything sounded gross. "Tofu Pizza?" I read out loud. "Soy Pizza, Sprouts Supreme, Veg — "

"I'm getting the sprouts," Dad said happily.

I checked the menu again. "Uh . . . I guess I'll try the Five-Grain Plain," I gulped.

"Good choice!" Dad smiled. He called the waitress over and ordered. "And give my daughter the Super Salad. She's in training," he added.

It took a long time for the food to come. By then I was really hungry. My Five-Grain Plain looked sort of like normal pizza. Maybe this won't be so bad, I thought. I thought wrong! It was horrible — it tasted like Play-Doh!

Daddy loved his Sprouts Supreme, though. He ordered two more slices and gobbled them up before I could finish my first. I would have washed it down with soda, but we didn't have any. We had celery juice instead. Lucky for me, Dad was still hungry. He ate the rest of my pizza while I picked at the salad.

When everything was finally gone, we walked back toward the car.

"Now can we go to the zoo?" I asked hopefully.

Dad looked at his watch. "It's getting kind of late," he said.

"But it's only seven-thirty," I protested. "The zoo doesn't close till nine."

"A champion gymnast needs her sleep," Dad said. "There will be lots of time for the zoo *after* you win that gold medal. And speaking of gold medals . . ." Daddy's voice trailed off as he unlocked the car. He reached into the backseat and handed me a big white box.

"What's this?" I asked.

"Take a look and see," he said.

I opened the box and gasped. Inside was a leotard. It was neon green with neon pink stripes and shiny gold sequins all over it. The whole thing was so bright it made my eyes hurt.

"So, what do you think?" Dad asked.

I think this is the ugliest leotard I've ever seen! I thought. But I didn't say that. I didn't say anything. I didn't know *what* to say.

"I wanted to get you something special for your competition," Dad said. "You'll really stand out in this!"

I took the leotard out of the box. It looked even uglier up close. I couldn't wear *this* to my competition. If I did, the judges would all go blind!

"B-But, Daddy," I said. "I — I . . ."

Dad grinned at me.

"I can't wear this at the meet," I blurted out. "I have to wear my regular uniform."

Now Dad looked disappointed. Oh, no! I didn't want to hurt his feelings.

"All the girls from my gym are supposed to look the same," I explained. "We're a team! Coach Jody says we should stand out because of our gymnastics — not our leotards."

Dad ran his finger over a sequined stripe. I could tell he really loved that leotard. "Well, at least you can wear it to practice," he said. "That'll show the other girls you mean business! Okay?"

I looked down at the leotard again. The sequins were all sparkly. They seemed to be looking back at me. Winking at me!

"Well, Katie?" Dad said. "What do you say?"

I looked from my dad to the leo and back again.

What he doesn't know won't hurt him, I thought. He'll never know I would rather die than wear that ugly leotard in public.

"Thanks, Daddy," I finally said. "It's great. I'll wear it tomorrow."

"I *knew* you'd like it!" He smiled and opened the car door for me. I climbed in and sat with the leotard on my lap.

Dad got in and started the car. He seemed happy, but I felt too awful to say anything else. I had just lied to my father! But it was better than *really* wearing the ugly leotard.

Suddenly Dad smiled and glanced over at me. "That leotard really brings out the green in your eyes," he said. "If Coach Jody doesn't mind, I think I'll come watch your practice tomorrow."

I gasped. "Y-you want to come to practice?"

"Definitely!" Dad said. "I can't wait to see my beautiful daughter in her beautiful new leotard!"

The Big Vault

"You have to come out of there some-time," Amanda yelled into the bathroom. "It's three-thirty. Time for warm-up."

"Come on, Katie," Dana coaxed. "We promise we won't laugh."

I took a deep breath and opened the door. My friends were all waiting outside the toilet stall where I'd been hiding for the last fifteen minutes.

I could feel my face turn pink. Bright pink. As pink and bright as the stripes on my hideously, horribly, totally terrible, super-ugly leotard.

"It's not that bad," Amanda said, picking a speck of lint off her leo. I could tell she was trying not to stare at me.

"It is so!" I looked at Amanda and sighed. It was Thursday again, and Amanda was wearing a beautiful pale lemon-yellow leotard. A beautiful *plain* pale lemon-yellow leotard!

"No, really, Katie," Dana said. "You look fine." Dana was in her old black leo. It had a big hole on the shoulder, a smaller one above her leg, and a faded gray splotch on her backside. I would have given anything to trade with her!

"Don't feel bad, Katie," Hannah Rose piped up. That made me feel *really* bad. Even Hannah Rose was being nice. She's *never* nice.

"I can't go out there," I insisted. "Everyone will laugh at me."

"But *we're* all in *here!*" Liz pointed out. "And nobody's laughing."

I looked around at my friends. Liz was right. No one was laughing. They all looked sorry for me. I felt sorry for me, too!

I sniffled. "You guys are being nice," I said. "But my dad is ruining everything! All he cares about is medals. Gold ones! He doesn't care anything about *me*. He — "

"Katie!" Dana gasped. "What are you talking about? Your dad *loves* you. He's been spending practically every minute with you since he came home from Mexico."

"Yeah," Amanda agreed. "So what if he wants you to win? I wish *my* father would be more like that."

"Well, I wish *mine* would just be normal," I muttered as I followed my friends into the gym.

Twenty minutes later, my ugly new leotard was soaked with sweat. But it wasn't because of the warm-up exercises. It was because I was nervous. I kept looking at the door, waiting for my dad to show up. I didn't want to mess up in front of him.

He still wasn't there when Coach Jody blew her whistle and said, "Junior gymnasts — on the mats." That's how she always ends warm-up. As I plopped down between Amanda and Dana, I began to relax. Maybe he wasn't coming after all.

"Okay, girls," Coach Jody announced, "this is our last workout before the big Level Five meet on Saturday."

As soon as she said *meet*, everyone started talking at once.

"Whoa!" Coach Jody said. "I'm glad you're all so excited. But now let's put that excitement to work. Today I want to concentrate on the vault."

As we marched over to the padded vaulting horse, I took one more peek at the door. This time my dad was there. He was wearing a gray tweed suit, a fancy shirt, and a tie. He looked very nice — and just a little bit dorky. For a minute, I almost forgot about my ugly leotard. I waved.

My father grinned and waved back. Then he mouthed something at me. It looked like *"Mice, knee, and toad!"*

"What?" I mouthed at him.

"MICE, KNEE, AND TOAD!" he mouthed again, only this time he moved his lips really slowly. He made faces. He looked like a crazy person. I glanced around to make sure no one else was watching. Then I mouthed "What?" again.

Before I could do anything to stop him, my father gave me another big smile and hollered "NICE LEOTARD" right out loud!

Everybody laughed at Dad. Even Coach Jody. I didn't blame them. I would have laughed, too — if I wasn't so embarrassed.

When everyone finally quieted down,

Coach Jody said, "Come on in, Mr. Magee. You're just in time." Then she said, "Katie, as long as your father is here, how would you like to go first?"

"Me?" I gulped. I definitely did not want to go first. I didn't even want to go last. I didn't want to go at all!

Everyone was looking at me.

"Okay," I said. I stepped up to the painted floor mark, took a deep breath, and ran toward the horse. I felt so nervous I was afraid I'd fall on my face. But somehow I landed on my feet.

"Not bad for starters," Coach Jody said with a smile.

That made me feel a little better. I glanced at Amanda and she gave me a thumbs-up.

But when I looked over at my dad, he was frowning.

"What's wrong?" I mouthed.

Still frowning, Dad pointed at me.

Then he pointed down to the floor. Or maybe to his shoes. I couldn't tell which.

"*What?*" I mouthed again.

"I think he wants you to keep your toes pointed," Dana whispered to me.

"Oh," I whispered back.

For my next vault, I concentrated really hard on my toes. I kept them pointed through my whole vault.

When I landed Coach Jody patted me on the back. "Much better, Katie," she told me. "Now I'd like to see just a little more extension."

"Okay," I said. Out of the corner of my eye, I caught a flash of gray tweed. My dad was waving at me. I tried to ignore him, but he just waved harder. He jogged along the bleachers, trying to get in front of me so I would see him. When I finally turned around, he pointed at his feet again.

Now what did he want me to do? My toes *were* pointed!

I shrugged at him and turned back to Coach Jody. "This time when you do your handstand, make believe you're trying to touch the ceiling with your toes," she said.

"Okay," I agreed.

As I got ready for my third vault, I could see my dad moving closer. I could feel his eyes on my back — it made me really nervous. Even so, I did a pretty good vault. I pointed my toes and imagined that they reached the ceiling.

"*Psst!*" my father hissed.

Oh, no, I thought. What now?

"*Psst!*" He did it again. Coach Jody frowned.

I shook my head and tried to shut out everything but Coach Jody's voice. "You've almost got it, kiddo — " she started.

"*PSST!*" Now the sound was really loud. Everyone turned to stare at Dad. Everyone but me. I looked down at the floor.

"Like this, Katie!" Dad called. "Do it like this!"

I heard Coach Jody gasp. She opened her mouth to say something, but it was too late.

My dad was already halfway to the horse!

Daddy hit the springboard with a loud *thunk!* — all 185 pounds of him. I gasped as he reached out for the horse and swung up into a beautiful handstand. Even with his brown lace-up shoes, I could see his toes were perfectly pointed. He kept them that way as he pushed off from the horse.

For one split second, he flew through the air. His striped tie fluttered in the breeze as he came back down. He totally nailed the landing, knees bent to absorb the shock. Then he straightened up and spread his arms to the sides.

There was a long moment of silence. Then Hannah Rose began to applaud. Liz giggled. Coach Jody looked shocked.

I ran out of the gym as fast as I could.

Dana and Amanda followed me into the locker room. By the time they got there, I had already yanked off my ugly new leotard. I sat down on the bench in my underwear and covered my face with my hands.

"This was the most embarrassing day of my whole life," I wailed. "And it's all my father's fault!" I scrunched up the ugly leotard and threw it on the floor. "He's acting completely crazy. First he makes me wear this horrible thing. Then *he* goes around doing gymnastics in a suit and a tie!"

Amanda reached into my locker and pulled out my nice old black leo. "I really like your dad," she said, handing it to me. "But maybe he *is* a little crazy."

"Well," Dana said with a grin. "He may be crazy — but he sure can vault!"

Too Many Coaches

Friday afternoon Amanda and I left school together, the way we always do.

"Do you want to sleep over tonight?" Amanda asked me as we headed for the bike racks.

"I can't," I said. "I'm going to my dad's. I have to say I'm sorry for running out of gym yesterday."

"Why?" Amanda cried. "*He's* the one who embarrassed *you!*"

"I know," I said. "But I shouldn't have left him there all alone. He didn't know that

I rode my bike home. Mom said he was really worried."

"Well, soon the meet will be over and your dad will stop doing vaults!" Amanda giggled.

"I can't believe the meet is tomorrow!" I said.

"Me neither," Amanda agreed. "Are you nervous?" she asked. But before I could answer, she handed me her backpack and started cartwheeling across the grass.

"Of course," I said, running to keep up. "You know how I get. Ner — "

" — vous!" Amanda finished for me as she bounced back to her feet. "Don't worry, Katie," she went on. "You'll be fine."

"I hope so," I said glumly. "My dad will be so mad if I don't win at least one gold medal. But I don't know if I can!"

"Hey, look!" Amanda said as we stopped at the bike racks. "Isn't that him over there?"

"Where?"

"There." Amanda pointed across the street.

I whirled around. Amanda was right. Dad's car was parked in front of the school, and he was standing next to it. He was talking to a short thin man with dark curly hair. They were both wearing warm-up suits and sneakers.

"Who's that other guy?" Amanda asked.

"I don't know," I said. "I never saw him before."

Suddenly my dad looked up and saw me. "Katie!" he called, waving both arms in the air. "Over here."

"You'd better go without me," I told Amanda. "Maybe my father came to take me to the zoo. He probably feels bad about embarrassing me yesterday."

"Okay," Amanda said, taking her pack

and dropping it into her bike basket. "Have fun," she yelled as she rode away.

"Thanks," I yelled back. "See you tomorrow." Then I wheeled my bike across the street.

"Hi, honey," Dad said. "Meet an old friend of mine, Paul Nelson. Paul — this is my daughter, Katie."

Mr. Nelson put out his hand, so I shook it.

"Glad to meet you, Katie," he said. "I've heard a lot about you."

"You have?" I gulped.

"You bet," he said with a smile. "Your dad says you're quite a gymnast."

I could feel myself blushing. I never know what to say when a grown-up says nice things about me. So I didn't say anything.

"Paul and I were on the same gymnastics team in college," my father explained.

"He was the star. Now he has his own gym in Holtsville."

"Wow!" I said. "Just like Coach Jody."

"Paul usually works with boys," Dad went on, "but as a special favor to me, he's agreed to take some time out today to give you a little one-on-one coaching."

"What?" I cried. "Why?"

"Well, you don't have much practice time left before your big meet," Dad said. "And Coach Jody is obviously too busy to give you the special attention you need."

"Why do I need special attention?" I cried. "Coach Jody gives me *lots* of attention. *She* thinks I'm doing okay without extra workouts!"

But Dad wasn't even listening. "So let's put your bike in the trunk," he said, "and we'll head over to Paul's gym. It's only half an hour away."

I couldn't believe it — all my father

cared about was winning a medal. I didn't move. I didn't want to go to some strange gym with a bunch of boys.

Dad looked surprised when I just stood there. "Wait until you see the place, Katie," he told me. "It's huge. You're going to love it."

"But, Daddy," I began. "I — "

"Come on, honey," he said, taking my bike from me. "We'll talk on the way — Paul's time is very valuable. With a little extra help, I'm sure you'll win at least one gold medal tomorrow. Maybe more," he added. "And if things really go well, we might even convince Paul to take you on full time."

"Take me on?" I yelped. "Full time? What are you talking about, Daddy?" I cried. "I already *have* a coach! I love Coach Jody, and I love her gym. All my friends are there. My whole team is there!"

I felt my face getting red again. But this time it wasn't because I was embarrassed. It was because I was mad.

"Calm down, Katie," Daddy said. "I'm only trying to help you win."

"Well, you're *not* helping," I said. "You're just making me feel bad. Ever since you got home, all you've done is make me feel bad. It's already Friday, and we haven't done any of the things *I* want to do. We haven't gone to the zoo. We haven't gone to the dog show. We haven't even — "

"But, Katie," my dad broke in. "I told you — we can do those things later. The meet is tomorrow. I just want to help you do your best."

"Then just stay away from my gym!" I yelled. "Stop bossing me around, and stop embarrassing me. You're ruining everything!"

I grabbed my bike away from him and pedaled off alone. I couldn't believe my own father was being so bossy! How could he want me to leave my coach and my gymnastics team?

I hope I don't win any medals at the stupid competition, I thought. *Then* Dad would stop talking about winning all the time.

But suddenly I had an awful idea. I told Dad to stay away from the gym. What if he *did* stay away?

What if he didn't come to my competition?

My Meet

"O-oh! say can you *seeeee,*
By the dawn's early *liiight* . . ."

As the Washington Elementary School glee club sang "The Star-Spangled Banner," I took my right hand down from my heart and squeezed Amanda's left hand. I was so nervous! Amanda squeezed back. I could tell she was nervous, too. Her hand was all sweaty.

It was twelve o'clock Saturday afternoon. The announcer had just introduced the teams — us, Central Gym, Riverdale, and Team Twist. As soon as the national anthem was over, the meet would begin.

I looked around the gym. The girls from all four teams were lined up facing the flag. I recognized most of them from our last meet, and that made me feel a little better. But then I looked at the bleachers, and I felt much worse.

I spotted Amanda's family right away. That was easy. The Calloways were way down in front, and they took up almost half of the row. Mom was right behind them. Dana's parents and Freddy were standing on one side of her. My dad should have been standing on her other side.

But he wasn't!

I knew it! I thought. Daddy isn't coming. And it's all my fault! I should never have yelled at him yesterday.

A minute later the glee club stopped singing and everyone sat down. It looked as if all the seats were filled.

All but one.

I stared down at the mats and told myself that Dad would come. He *had* to!

When I looked up again, he was there! My dad was squeezing his way between the rows of seats. I grinned and waved at him. But Daddy didn't wave back.

I guess he's still mad, I thought.

Just as Daddy sat down, the announcer's voice blared over the loudspeaker: "Level Five gymnasts! Take your places. The meet will now begin."

Coach Jody had already given us the order of events — balance beam, uneven parallel bars, vault, and floor exercise — and our places in it. I would go after Amanda, Hannah Rose, and Dana.

As I sat on the bench watching my friends do their beam routines, I got more and more nervous. Dana was almost perfect. She got 9.7! If only I could be that good —

if only I could win a gold medal. My dad would be so proud of me!

Finally, it was my turn. I could feel Daddy's eyes on my back as I mounted the beam.

Don't think about him, I thought, going into my backward swing turn. Don't think about falling. Don't think —

The next thing I knew, I was down on the floor. I hadn't even completed my first move and I had already fallen off the beam! As I hopped back on, I caught a glimpse of my father's face. He frowned. I didn't blame him.

For the rest of my routine, I just concentrated on staying on the beam. I managed not to fall off again, but I felt kind of stiff and wobbly.

Everyone clapped when I finished, even my father. And when I marched back to the bench, my teammates all hugged me.

But I felt terrible. I knew they were only being nice to me — they felt sorry for me. My score was 7.3.

"Don't worry, Katie," Amanda said. "You still have three more chances to win a medal."

"Amanda's right," Dana said. "You'll do much better on the uneven parallel bars."

But Amanda was wrong. And so was Dana. I didn't do better on the uneven bars. I did worse. I fell off *twice*! Both times I picked myself up and got back on. When I finally finished my routine, I didn't look up at my dad. I didn't even look at the scoreboard. I already knew how I'd done. Terrible!

When it came time for my vault, all I could think about was Daddy's suit-and-tie vault. I took a deep breath and stepped up to the mark.

Watch your toes! I told myself as I

ran toward the horse. Watch your toes!

I pointed my toes as I bounced off the springboard, and I kept them pointed for the whole vault. I hope Daddy's watching, I thought just before I landed. And then, with all ten toes perfectly pointed, I came down — SPLAT! — flat on my behind!

This time, when I got back to the bench, my teammates just patted me on the back. I sat down between Dana and Amanda and watched the other girls do their vaults.

Then it was my turn again.

The fourth and final event was the floor exercise. I couldn't wait to do my routine. I wanted this whole awful competition to be over. When Hannah Rose finished her routine, I walked over to the mats and waited for the signal to begin. I didn't feel nervous — I'd *already* messed up my beam, uneven bars, and vault routines. I couldn't do any worse on the floor. At least there was nothing to fall off of!

I closed my eyes and went over my whole floor routine in my mind:

Body wave; dive cartwheel; round-off, flic-flac, flic-flac, step out; 360-degree turn; back walkover; split leap; front handspring, round-off, back extension roll; hitch kick, handstand, and forward roll.

"Katie Magee, Jody's Gym." The announcer's voice rang over the loud-speaker. I opened my eyes and stepped onto the mat. I didn't think of my father. I didn't think of the score. I didn't think of anything. I just went out and did my routine — exactly the way I had pictured it!

When I finished, the audience clapped for a long time — as if they really meant it. And when I saw my score, I knew they did.

I got a 9.2! That wasn't as good as a girl from Riverdale's 9.5, and it wasn't as good as Amanda's 9.3. But it was good enough for a bronze medal.

I just hoped it was good enough for my dad.

In the locker room, my teammates crowded around Amanda. She wore two bronze medals and one silver around her neck. Every time she moved, they made a clanking sound.

"Can I try one on?" Emily asked.

"Sure," Amanda said, slipping a bronze medal over her head.

"Me, too?" Liz asked.

Amanda handed her the other bronze.

Hannah Rose just smiled. She had her own medal — a silver one for the vault.

"I wonder if I'll ever win any medals," Liz said wistfully.

"Of course you will," Amanda said.

"Not if *you* keep hogging them all!" Dana joked, high-fiving Amanda. "Three medals!" she exclaimed. "I am *so* jealous." She didn't look it, though. She looked really happy with the one *gold* medal she won for beam. Everyone looked really happy.

I knew I should be happy, too. My team won the all-around championship, and I won a medal of my own. But all I could think of was Dad.

He wanted me to win a gold.

He must be so disappointed in me.

Who's #1?

I showered and changed as slowly as I could. I even washed my hair and folded up my gym clothes. But I knew I'd have to face my father sometime.

Or would I?

Suddenly a terrible thought came into my head. Maybe my dad wasn't even waiting outside for me! Maybe he was still mad that I'd yelled at him yesterday. Maybe he was mad that I hadn't won a gold medal. What if he didn't even want to see me?

I grabbed my gym bag and ran out of the locker room.

There were still a lot of people standing around in the hallway — mostly
gymnasts from the other teams and their
families. Everyone seemed to be talking and
laughing at once.

I looked up and down the hall. Dana
and her parents were just leaving. Freddy
was wearing Dana's gold medal around his
neck. But I didn't see anyone else I knew.
Not even my mom.

Suddenly, a familiar voice boomed out:
"How about a big hug from my little girl?"

"Daddy!"

I flew across the room and into my
father's arms. Then I squeezed him with all
my might. I was so happy to see him.

"That was some hug," he said when I
finally let go. "And that was some perfor-
mance. Your floor exercise was great!" He
bent down so his face was right next to
mine. "Do you have any idea how proud I
am of you?" he asked.

"You're not mad that I didn't win any gold medals?" I asked.

"Of course not," he said. "The last I heard, *you* were mad at *me*! I phoned your mom last night after you were asleep and we had a long talk about you. She — "

"Hey, where *is* Mom?" I blurted out.

"Your mother went home," Daddy said. "She thought you and I needed to do some talking, too."

"Oh, Daddy!" I cried. "I'm so sorry I yelled at you yesterday. I didn't mean — "

"Hold on, honey," my father interrupted. "You don't have to apologize. You had every right to be angry. *I'm* the one who should apologize," he said, standing up straight again. "I haven't been much fun since I came home, have I?"

"Well . . ." I began. I could feel my face turning pink.

"I know it's true," Daddy said. "I didn't mean to be pushy. I just wanted to be close to you. Almost all your letters were about gymnastics, so I figured that was the way to do it."

"But we *are* close," I told him. "I love you."

"I missed almost half a year of your life," Dad said. "That's a lot of lost time to make up for."

"Well, you don't have to make it all up in one week!" I told him.

Daddy reached down and ruffled my hair. "Maybe I did get a little carried away," he said. "But I was only trying to help. I thought you *wanted* to win a gold medal."

"I did," I admitted. "I still do! But I want to stay with my team. And I want to do fun stuff with you."

Dad let out a big sigh. "Whew!" he said. "That's a relief!"

"Whew!" I agreed.

Suddenly I was so happy I felt like doing handsprings. So I did one!

As soon as I bounced back to my feet, Daddy did one, too. Then we both laughed.

"Well, now that we've got that out of our system," Dad said, "I have a little present for you."

Uh-oh! I thought. "It's not another leotard, is it?" I asked.

"Don't worry," Daddy said as he pulled a tiny package out of his pocket and handed it to me. "I think you'll like this."

I tore off the wrapping paper and opened the black velvet box. A shiny gold charm on a long gold chain was nestled inside. The charm was a circle about the size of a quarter, with some of the gold cut away. The part that was still left said *#1*.

"Do you like it, Katie?" Daddy asked.

"I love it!" I replied. "It's great! But I'm not *really* number one. Today I was only number three."

My father smiled as he took the necklace out of my hand and fastened it around

my neck. Then he gave me another hug. "Well, you're my number one daughter!"

"And you're my number one dad," I said, hugging him back. "Oh, Daddy! I'm so glad you're home!"

"I am, too," my father said. "Now how about that trip to the zoo?" he asked. "I think we've kept those three little bears waiting long enough."

"Great idea," I said. I tucked my gold #1 charm under my collar and smiled at my dad. "I'll race you to the car!"

Stand up and cheer!

JUNIOR GYMNASTS

by Teddy Slater
illustrated by Wayne Alfano

**Teammates Dana, Katie, and Amanda
love gymnastics, competitions, and <u>friendship</u>!**

☆	BBY85997-8	Junior Gymnasts #1: Dana's Competition	$2.99
☆	BBY85998-6	Junior Gymnasts #2: Katie's Big Move	$2.99
☆	BBY85999-4	Junior Gymnasts #3: Amanda's Perfect 10	$2.99
☆	BBY86003-8	Junior Gymnasts #4: Dana's Best Friend	$2.99
☆	BBY95987-5	Junior Gymnasts #5: Katie's Gold Medal	$2.99

JUNIOR GYMNASTS

The big meet is on Friday the 13th. How can superstitious Amanda ever compete, much less win?

Amanda is totally superstitious. She even has special things that she *has* to do before each meet. So when an important competition is on this unlucky day, Amanda thinks there's no way she'll be able to perform. Can her teammates prove to Amanda that she doesn't need luck to be the best gymnast?

Junior Gymnasts # 6
Amanda's Unlucky Day
by Teddy Slater

Coming to a bookstore near you.

JRG